儿童情绪管理与性格

MOM I CAN DO IT

妈妈我能行

胡媛媛 编

广东旅游出版社
GUANGDONG TRAVEL & TOURISM PRESS
中国·广州

图书在版编目（ＣＩＰ）数据

妈妈我能行 / 胡媛媛编. — 广州：广东旅游出版社, 2016.11
（儿童情绪管理与性格培养绘本）
ISBN 978-7-5570-0546-7

Ⅰ. ①妈… Ⅱ. ①胡… Ⅲ. ①儿童故事 – 图画故事 – 中国 – 当代 Ⅳ. ①I287.8

中国版本图书馆 CIP 数据核字(2016)第 237816 号

总 策 划：罗艳辉
责任编辑：殷如筠
封面绘图：徐武祥
责任技编：刘振华
责任校对：李瑞苑

妈 妈 我 能 行
MAMA　WO　NENG　XING

广东旅游出版社出版发行
（广州市越秀区建设街道环市东路 338 号银政大厦西楼 12 楼　　邮编：510030）
邮购电话：020-87348243
广东旅游出版社图书网
www.tourpress.cn
湖北楚天传媒印务有限责任公司
（湖北省武汉市东湖新技术开发区流芳园横路 1 号　　邮编：430205）
787 毫米 × 1092 毫米　16 开　2 印张　1 千字
2016 年 11 月第 1 版第 1 次印刷
定价：15.00 元

小熊一天天在长大。

Little Bear is growing up day by day.

妈妈帮他穿小袜。

Mother bear helps him to put on socks.

"妈妈妈妈我能行。看，我会自己穿小袜！"

"Mom, I can do it. Look, I can put on my socks by myself!"

小熊穿上外套，自己扣纽扣。

Little Bear puts on his coat and buttons up.

"妈妈，我能自己扣好！"小熊边说
边扣好了纽扣。

"Mom, I can button up by myself!"
Little Bear buttons up nicely.

要下楼梯了,妈妈想抱小熊。

They are going to walk down the stairs. Mother bear wants to take Little Bear in her arms.

"不，不，我要自己下。哈哈，妈妈，
我下到你前面了。"

*"No, no. I can walk by myself.
Ha-ha, mom, I walked over you!"*

妈妈做晚餐，黄瓜炒鸡蛋。

Mother bear is making dinner,
fried eggs with cucumbers.

"小黄瓜，你听话，我来给你洗澡吧。"

"Little cucumber, be good, let me give you a bath."

"妈妈妈妈,小黄瓜洗干净了。"
"啊,宝宝真是顶呱呱!"

"Mom, I washed the cucumber clean."
"Wow, baby, you are excellent!"

妈妈头晕晕。哎呀，妈妈生病了，小熊宝宝急得快哭了。

Mother bear feels dizzy. Oh, mom gets sick. Little Bear gets panic and cries.

宝宝你别哭，你能帮帮妈妈吗？"

"Don't cry, baby. Can you help me?"

"妈妈妈妈我能行！"

"I can, mom!"

"你给妈妈倒杯水吧。"

"Can you please give me a cup of water?"

小口杯，洗一洗，小茶壶，提手里。我先尝一尝，不烫也不凉。"好妈妈，请喝茶。"

Little Bear washes a cup and makes tea. He tastes the tea to make sure it's neither too hot, nor too cold. "Dear mom, have some tea."

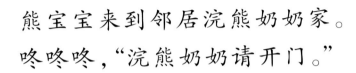

熊宝宝来到邻居浣熊奶奶家。

咚咚咚,"浣熊奶奶请开门。"

Little Bear goes to the neighbor grandma raccoon's house.

Knock, knock, knock. "Grandma Raccoon, could you please open the door?"

"小熊宝贝，什么事儿啊？"

"What's going on, my baby bear?"

"妈妈生病了，请您快快去我家。"

"My mom got sick, please come to my home."

浣熊奶奶给妈妈吃了药。

Grandma Raccoon gives some medicine to mother bear.

妈妈睡着了。

Mom falls asleep.

小熊宝宝坐在床边陪妈妈，直到爸爸回了家。

Little Bear sits by bedside to look after mom until dad comes back.

爸爸把小熊宝宝举高高："宝宝能照顾妈妈了，真行！"

小熊宝宝得到了夸奖，笑呀笑哈哈。

Dad holds him up and says, "you can take care of your mom, baby. You did good!"

Little Bear laughs happily on hearing of the praise.

给父母的话：

在父母眼里，孩子是无价之宝，怎么呵护都不为过。替孩子穿衣、喂饭、收拾玩具……父母巴不得一生都替孩子当贴身保姆，却不知道过分溺爱恰似一条锁链，锁住了孩子自理能力、创造能力的发展，锁住了孩子天生的那颗感知生活，于生活中获得自尊、自信的心灵。

睿智的教育专家很早就告诉为人父母者：世界上所有的爱都以聚合为目的，只有亲子之爱是以分离为目的。父母对孩子放手得越早，孩子的独立能力就越强；孩子今后飞得越高，父母的亲子教育就越成功。你看，绘本中的小熊宝宝，从自己穿袜子、自己扣扣子、自己下楼梯学起，一点一点获得了生活的体验，获得了"成功"的满足和信心，最后当妈妈突然病倒，也能像模像样地照顾好妈妈，这就是成长的喜悦。

让孩子"能行"，父母可以试试从以下几个方面入手：

1. 给孩子知情权。对周围世界的了解和认识，是孩子迈向独立自主的第一步。2. 尊重孩子对物品的所有权。父母对孩子给出足够的尊重，孩子才会生出相应的责任感，要给孩子机会去体验独立完成的感觉。3. 给孩子选择权。孩子选择的本领是要通过真的做选择才能学会的。4. 进行后果教育。让孩子学会总结、学会吸取教训，这也是取代惩罚的办法。5. 学会规划和预期。让孩子树立意识，能让他们学习控制自己的生活。6. 少命令少指责多鼓励。7. 给孩子安全感。孩子有了安全感，才敢于去冒险尝试，才敢于去承担责任。